PURR-FECTLY LUCKY

Kimberly Palmucci

Illustrated by Brandi McCann

One warm, bright morning,
on a day much like today,
the sun was busy waking up;
the moon was yawning away.

Birds began their chirping;
the sun began to swelter.
All the animals welcomed
a new day in the shelter.

These pets were like all others;
they loved to play, romp, and roam.
But they lived inside the shelter,
waiting for a family and a home.

The animals awoke to the sunlight,
a new day bringing fresh hope to claim.
One cat was especially hopeful;
Lucky was his name!

Lucky was just like the others;
he loved to frolic, meow, and play.
He climbed, he jumped, he ran so fast,
welcoming the sun with a smile each day.

But Lucky was also different,
and for that, he received mostly pity.
He was missing a leg – he was special.
Lucky was a three-legged kitty.

Each sunrise brought new faces,
peering into his cage each day.
"Look—how cute!...but he's missing a leg;
let's get one who can run and play."

"But I can run and play, too!"

Other pets were given new homes,
but Lucky was left feeling blue.
If everyone thought being different was bad,
he had to start believing it, too.

9

"Why can't I be like the others?
Being perfect like them—if only!
No one wants a three-legged cat;
being different is ever so lonely."

But one day the sun was especially bright,
a new morning with a new surprise.
A new cat had arrived next to Lucky's cage,
a kind face that looked older and wise.

11

"Why so blue, little one?" the wise cat asked.
"Your eyes look lonely and sad.
You have so much living to do still!
So much fun and play to be had."

Lucky sighed and looked at the floor.
"Thanks, but don't you see?
I'm missing a leg, and I'm different;
no one wants a cat like me."

13

"Nonsense!" exclaimed the wise cat.
"You know nothing of what you speak.
Being different is not a bad thing;
it makes you special, interesting, unique!"

14

"Having three legs makes you stand out;
you're amazing—don't you see?
You are smart and brave like no other!
And you'll find the perfect family."

15

Lucky looked at his missing leg,
and then at the wise elder cat.
"You are right! I'm special! I'm purr-fect!"
And he smiled at the thought of that.

The sun arose on a new day,
and Lucky awoke with a smile.
Because after waiting for so long,
a family walked toward him down the aisle.

They looked in his cage, and into his eyes,
"You are perfect, and you are strong.
We've been looking for a cat like you;
in our family is where you belong."

After years of happy sunrises,
Lucky looked at his family and knew:
they chose him because he was special;
the words of his wise friend were true.

Unique is strong, and different is good!
While sometimes a challenge, it's true.
Everyone's made in their own special way;
be proud to be purr-fectly you!

20

The End

Made in the USA
Columbia, SC
10 November 2018